Popcorn ELT Readers

Meet ... everyone from

Po is a panda. He works in his dad's noodle shop. He loves kung fu, but he isn't very good at it.

Po's dad has got a noodle shop. His noodles are special.

Po's dad

Po

Master Shifu is a great kung fu teacher. He lives at the Jade Palace.

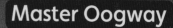

Master Oogway

Master Shifu

Master Oogway is a very old kung fu teacher. He knows a lot of things.

The Furious Five

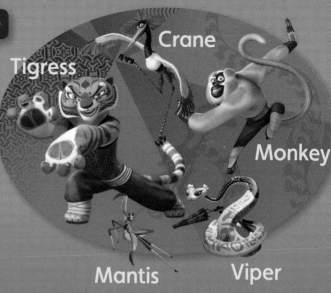

The Furious Five are very good at kung fu. They all want to be the Dragon Warrior.

Tigress

Crane

Monkey

Mantis

Viper

Tai Lung

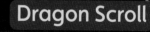

Dragon Scroll

Every fighter would like to be the **Dragon Warrior**. The **Dragon Scroll** is a very special book. It helps the Dragon Warrior.

Tai Lung is in prison. He wants to be the Dragon Warrior, but no one wants this.

Before you read ...
What do you think?
Who is going to be the Dragon Warrior?

New Words

What do these new words mean? Ask your teacher or use your dictionary.

fight / fighter

The girls are **fighting**.
They are good **fighters**.

escape

He's **escaping**! Stop him!

fireworks

She likes watching **fireworks**.

fat

The dog is very **fat**.

hit

Hit it!

noodles

These are **noodles**.

people

There are four **people**.

prison

He's in **prison**.

special

He's got a **special** drink.

win

She is **winning**.

'I've got an idea!'

I've got an idea!

Verbs

Present	Past
fall	fell
fight	fought
win	won

CHAPTER ONE
The Dragon Warrior

Master Oogway was at the Jade Palace in China.

'I think that Tai Lung is going to escape from prison,' Oogway said.

Master Shifu was frightened.

'What can we do?' he asked.

'I'm going to find a new Dragon Warrior. The Dragon Warrior can fight Tai Lung.'

Everyone in town ran to the Jade Palace.

'Come and watch!' they shouted. 'We're going to have a new Dragon Warrior!'

'Wow!' said Po. Po loved watching kung fu. 'I'm coming too!' He didn't want to work today.

'Wait, Po!' his dad shouted. 'Take these noodles with you. People always want to buy noodles.'

The people watched the kung fu of the Furious
Five: Tigress, Crane, Mantis, Monkey and Viper.
It was great!

'Who is going to be the Dragon Warrior?'
everyone asked.

Po went to the Jade Palace. He went slowly because he was fat and he had a lot of noodles. He was late.

'Open the door!' he shouted, but no one answered.

Po found some fireworks.

'These can help me!' he said.

With the fireworks under him, he went up and up. Then he fell down and down.

'Aaaarrrr!' he shouted.

When Po opened his eyes, he was in the Jade Palace. He was next to the Furious Five and Master Oogway.

'You!' Oogway said to Po. 'You are the Dragon Warrior.'

'Me?' said Po.

Master Shifu and the Furious Five were not happy.

CHAPTER TWO
Kung fu classes

Po started kung fu classes with Master Shifu.
Shifu and the Furious Five laughed.

'You're fat!' Shifu said. 'You can't win a fight
with Tai Lung.'

Po had a lot of classes with Master Shifu. He fell again and again, but he didn't stop. He wanted to be good at kung fu. He didn't want to work in the noodle shop again.

'He's bad at kung fu,' Tigress said, 'but he works and works.'

After this, the Furious Five and Po were friends.

Po made noodles for the Furious Five.

'These are nice!' they said.

'They're OK, but my dad's noodles are great. He puts something special in them,' Po said.

'What is it?'

'I don't know,' Po answered.

Shifu came in.

'Tai Lung escaped from prison yesterday!' he said. 'He's coming here!'

'We can fight Tai Lung!' the Furious Five said.

'No,' Shifu said. 'Po is the Dragon Warrior. Po is going to fight him.'

CHAPTER THREE
Fighting for noodles

Po was frightened. When he was frightened, he was always hungry.

'What can I eat?' he said. He went to the kitchen. He looked everywhere. He jumped on the table. He opened doors with his feet.

Master Shifu watched him.

'You're very good at kung fu when you want to eat! I've got an idea,' he said.

The next day, Master Shifu had some noodles. Po was hungry and he fought Master Shifu for the noodles. They fought and fought. Soon Po was good at kung fu!

Tigress wanted to fight Tai Lung.

'I can win!' she said.

Her friends went with her. They all wanted to help.

They all fought Tai Lung, but Tai Lung won.

'You ... all of you ... are nothing,' Tai Lung laughed. 'I want to fight someone special. I want to fight the Dragon Warrior.'

The Furious Five went back to the Jade Palace.

'We didn't win,' Tigress said. 'And now Tai Lung is coming to the town.'

Po was frightened.

'Read the Dragon Scroll,' Master Shifu said. 'It can help you.'

Po opened the Scroll. Everyone watched.

'Oh no!' he said. 'There's nothing in the Scroll. I can't fight Tai Lung!'

'Help the people in the town,' Master Shifu shouted. 'I'm going to fight Tai Lung!'

Po and the Furious Five went to the town.

'Tai Lung is coming,' they said to everyone.
'Come with us!'

Po saw his dad.

'Don't be sad, Po,' his dad said.

'You can make great noodles, but I can't,' Po
said. 'And I'm not a good Dragon Warrior.'

'There's nothing special in my noodles,' Po's dad said. 'Why are my noodles great? Because everyone thinks that they are special!'

Po looked at the Dragon Scroll again. There was nothing on it.

'Now I understand!' Po said. 'It's me! I am special and I can fight Tai Lung!'

He ran to the Jade Palace.

CHAPTER FOUR
'Give the Scroll to me!'

Tai Lung was at the Jade Palace. He hit Master Shifu again and again.

Suddenly Po was there. The Dragon Scroll was in his hand.

'I'm the Dragon Warrior!' he shouted.

Tai Lung laughed. 'You? You're fat! You can't win! Soon I'm going to be the Dragon Warrior. Give the Scroll to me!'

'No!' Po shouted.

They fought for the Dragon Scroll.

'I can fight for noodles, and I can fight for this,' Po said.

They fought in the Jade Palace and they fought in the town.

Po's kung fu was great. He won! Everyone was very happy.

Then Po ran to the Jade Palace.

'Are you OK, Master Shifu?' Po asked. But Shifu said nothing.

Po was very sad.

Suddenly Shifu opened his eyes.

'I'm OK, Po,' he said. 'And you are a great Dragon Warrior!'

THE END

IT COMES FROM CHINA!

Kung fu comes from China. Read about
more things that come from China.

Kung fu

Kung fu started in China a long time ago. There are a lot of types of kung fu. Some types of kung fu have animal names: Tiger, Crane, Dragon, Monkey, Mantis and Viper. People now do kung fu around the world.

Paper

2000 years ago, people in China made the world's first paper. They made books, tea bags and banknotes. Old Chinese books were scrolls.

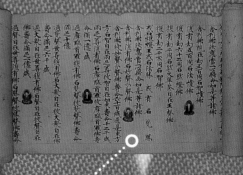

scroll

China

Fireworks

The world's first fireworks were Chinese. Today 80% of the world's fireworks come from China. You can see a lot of fireworks at Chinese New Year.

Chinese dragon

In China, the dragon is very strong and very lucky.

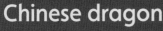

★
What things come from your country?
★

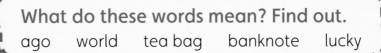

What do these words mean? Find out.
ago   world   tea bag   banknote   lucky

After you read

1 Match the people and descriptions.

a) Master Oogway

b) Master Shifu

c) Po

d) Tai Lung

e) Tigress

i) He works in a noodle shop.

ii) He escapes from prison.

iii) He is Po's kung fu teacher.

iv) She is one of the Furious Five.

v) He thinks that Tai Lung is going to escape.

2 True(✓) or False (✗)? Write in the box.

a) Po likes watching kung fu. ☑

b) Po likes noodles. ☐

c) Master Oogway is in prison. ☐

d) Master Shifu is a great teacher. ☐

e) Tigress is the Dragon Warrior. ☐

f) The Furious Five fight Tai Lung. ☐

g) Tai Lung reads the Dragon Scroll. ☐

h) Po fights Tai Lung and wins. ☐

Where's the popcorn?
**Look in your book.
Can you find it?**

28

Puzzle time!

1 Who or what is it? Write next to each picture.

a) Master ......Shifu......

b) the ....

c) Po's ....

d) some ....

2 Match two speech bubbles to each picture.

a) (I'm hungry.)

b) (I'm angry.)

c) (I'm frightened.)

d) (I'm going up and up.)

e) (I'm going to fight the Dragon Warrior.)

f) (These noodles are great.)

3 Put the letters in order and write the word under the correct picture.

nosirp ~~paeces~~ dolseno loeepp

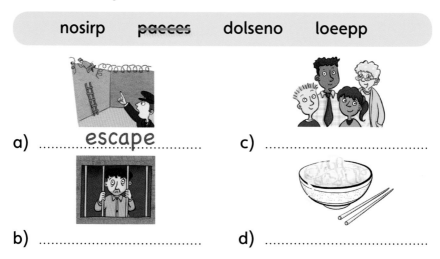

a) .... escape ....   c) ....

b) ....   d) ....

4 How many can you see? Count and write.

a) .....5.... heads   b) .... eyes   c) .... fighters

d) .... legs   e) .... animals with 'm' in their names

Imagine...

1 Work in pairs. Choose a character.

Tai Lung

Po

Shifu

Tigress

Monkey

2 Mime the character. Your friends guess who you are.

Look at my kung fu!

You're Po!

Chant

1 [T 8] **Listen and read.**

Tai Lung and Po

Tai Lung is very bad
And Po is very fat.
Tai Lung can do kung fu.
He's very good at that.

Tai Lung escapes from prison.
He comes to town. Oh no!
He fights the Dragon Warrior.
Who wins the fight? It's Po!

2 [T 9] **Say the chant.**